There's a Ship
Outside My Window

Story by Mike Lefroy
Illustrations by Loma Tilders

PM Library

Ruby Level 27 Set A

U.S. Edition © 2006 Harcourt Achieve Inc.
10801 N. MoPac Expressway
Building #3
Austin, TX 78759
www.harcourtachieve.com

Text © 2001 Cengage Learning Australia Pty Limited
Illustrations © 2001 Cengage Learning Australia Pty Limited
Originally published in Australia by Cengage Learning Australia

8 9 10 11 12 13 14   1957   13 12 11 10 09
4500205010

Text: Mike Lefroy
Illustrations: Loma Tilders
Printed in China by 1010 Printing International Ltd

There's a Ship Outside My Window
ISBN 978 0 76 357790 2

Contents

Chapter 1	A Shed for a Ship	4
Chapter 2	From Faraway Forests	7
Chapter 3	*Duyfken's* Story	9
Chapter 4	Bending with Fire	16
Chapter 5	Taking Shape	18
Chapter 6	Finishing Touches	24
Chapter 7	Ready for Adventure	27
	Glossary	32

A Shed for a Ship

The first thing I do when I get up in the morning is look out at the sea. It's always there, a patch of blue next to the old museum.

From my home I can walk to the beach in a couple of minutes. I cross the one-way street and the lawn in front of the museum, go over the railroad track, and pass the circling seagulls dive-bombing for scraps of food. Then I'm there, looking out to the long, blue horizon.

But one morning I didn't even notice the sea. Something very strange was happening right below my window. There were people everywhere. Some were working with a machine to scoop up the lawn in front of the museum and load it into a truck. Others were unloading building materials and hammering in posts.

The next day, three large trucks arrived and began pumping concrete over the place where the lawn used to be. I wandered down to take a look.

"What are you building?" I asked the man wearing a yellow hard hat.

"A shed. We're laying this concrete for the floor," he replied.

"What's the shed for?" I asked.

"A ship," he answered.

Chapter 2

From Faraway Forests

Within a couple of weeks a skeleton of gray metal appeared on the concrete floor. It was soon covered by a layer of yellow tin. Finally the shed was finished and I couldn't see the sea anymore from my window.

"Don't worry," said Mom. "The shed won't be there forever. And when it comes down, you will see a beautiful ship."

I was beginning to get used to the idea of having a ship outside my window.

A rumbling truck delivered the first part of the ship. I stood and watched the crane as it lifted the huge logs and stacked them next to the shed.

"These logs are from oak trees that grew in a forest on the other side of the world," said Bill, the chief shipbuilder, who was guiding the logs into position. "When they leave here they will be part of the ship and able to sail away by themselves."

Chapter 3

Duyfken's Story

Inside the shed, preparations were being made for building the ship. Wooden blocks were placed down the middle of the floor and large pieces of timber were lifted onto them. Then they were all joined together.

I followed Bill around as he helped the other shipbuilders move the wood into position. He walked so fast I had to run to keep up, but whenever I asked him a question he always stopped to answer me.

One time he looked at me with a smile, picked up a piece of wood from the floor and then, taking a pencil from behind his ear, drew me a picture.

"That's the keel of the ship—it's just like your backbone," explained Bill. He drew a picture of me lying in the shed as though I was the bottom of the ship. "We'll make our ship's backbone strong and straight like yours so that *Duyfken* will sail fast and true."

I ran my hand down my back and felt the lumpy bones of my spine.

Every day after school I would go to the shed. Sometimes I helped Captain Jim sweep up the sawdust. Sometimes I carried tools for the shipbuilders. And sometimes I just sat and watched the artist who was painting a huge mural of an old harbor.

One day Bill told me a story.

"Many years ago, a little ship, just like this one we're building, left that harbor on a voyage of adventure," said Bill, pointing up to the painting. "The ship was built in Holland, where the name, *Duyfken*, means "little dove." The job of the little ship was to sail out in front of the fleet and bring back news from far beyond the horizon."

"But *Duyfken*'s most famous voyage was when the little ship sailed on its own. For weeks, the crew sailed through calm and storms looking for gold and other treasures. They saw many islands, and met many people who lived lives so different from their own that they often struggled to understand one another.

Sometimes they exchanged gifts, but at other times, the people who lived in these places were very unhappy that the sailors had come to their lands. This led to fighting more than once."

"The *Duyfken* returned to port without the treasures the crew were seeking. All they had were words in a journal and a map of their journey. What they didn't realize was that they had started to chart the great continent now called Australia. The map was their treasure."

"What happened to the ship?" I asked.

"One day it was taken ashore to be repaired," said Bill. "But the ship's back had been broken by too many storms and battles, and *Duyfken* never went to sea again."

I had my next question ready. "Will this *Duyfken* go to sea?"

"Most certainly," Bill replied. "But first we need to add something extra to the backbone. Come and I'll show you."

Chapter 4

Bending with Fire

We walked outside the shed where one of the workers, Barney, was starting a fire.

"How does a fire help build a ship?" I wondered aloud.

"You'll just have to wait and see," said Barney with a wink, as he added another piece of oak to the flames.

For the next few months I woke up each morning to the smell of wood smoke curling over the fence and past my window.

"This is the way they built a ship in the old days," said Barney, as I helped him stoke the fire underneath a long plank of wood.

"Won't it just burn right through?" I asked, pointing to the blackened surface of the wood.

"We only let the fire scorch the outside of the plank," said Barney. "That makes the wood soft enough so we can bend it without breaking it."

Chapter 5

Taking Shape

Inside the shed, the lower part of the ship began to look like a long curved dish as the planks of scorched wood were joined to the keel.

The next job was to strengthen the hull by laying large pieces of timber across the planks to hold them together.

"These are like our ribs," said Bill, tapping his chest. "They will make the ship strong enough to sail through any storm."

"How do you know what *Duyfken* looked like?" I asked Bill.

"We will never know exactly," he said. "The old shipbuilders carried the plans in their heads and just told the other shipbuilders what they wanted. They didn't draw plans like we do. Luckily, we have some tiny pictures of *Duyfken* to help us."

He opened a book to a detailed drawing of a fleet in port. "That's it—the little one," he said, pointing to the smallest ship.

"This picture tells us what *Duyfken* looked like on the water. We also have clues from ships' journals and paintings of other ships. They all make it possible for us to draw these." Bill rolled a large plan out on the table. "That's the next piece we'll make. It's called the rudder. It will help to steer the ship."

As *Duyfken* grew toward the roof of the shed, different pieces of timber were shaped on the floor. Chunks of oak and eucalyptus from local forests were made into supports for the decks. Long, straight pieces of pine were transformed into the masts and spars that would hold up the sails.

Hundreds of slender, oak broomsticks were cut about a yard long and laid out ready to hold the ship together.

"They used to call these tree nails," said Captain Jim. "They are like the nails we use now—only made of wood."

I wrote my name on a nail and watched Captain Jim drive it right through the ship to pin the plank onto the rib. He let me hammer a wooden wedge into a slit in the end to make the tree nail head swell and hold it firmly in place.

"So now you're part of the ship, too," Captain Jim laughed, wiping the sweat from his forehead with the back of his sleeve.

As the tree nails were being driven into the hull, the planks were smoothed and made ready for the caulking.

"We need to fill those gaps between the planks so that the ship doesn't leak," said Captain Jim. "We want *Duyfken* to be a ship, not a submarine."

Chapter 6

Finishing Touches

It didn't seem long before *Duyfken* had grown so much that it was almost too big for the shed. The hull and decks were nearly finished and the gun ports for the cannon around the side of the ship were ready for action. The hull glistened with clear varnish and bright strips of color had been added to the bow and the stern.

In the corner of the shed a woodcarver named Jenny bent over her workbench, putting the finishing touches on carved pieces that would decorate *Duyfken*.

At one end of the shed, Rick and his helpers were working on the bow of the ship. At the other end, Danny and his team were putting the finishing touches on the high, wooden wall that formed the stern of the ship.

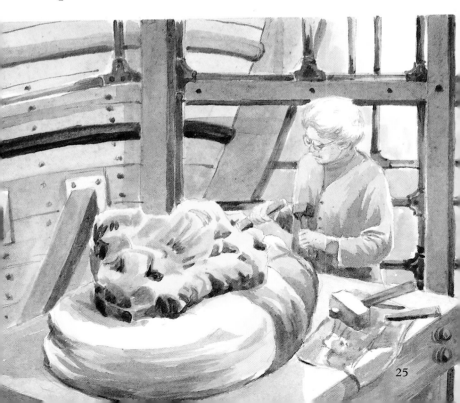

"Where's the steering wheel?" I asked Danny.

"It hadn't been invented when *Duyfken* sailed," he said. "They used a lever called a whipstaff. You pushed it from side to side and it would turn the rudder. That's it down there."

"How did they see where they were going?" I asked, peering into the darkness.

"The person at the helm just followed instructions from the captain up on the deck."

Danny let me climb down and stand next to the whipstaff. I held the thick, wooden pole, ready for my orders.

"Your dad wants you home for dinner," called Danny.

Those were not the instructions I was hoping for.

Chapter 7

Ready for Adventure

Down by the harbor, in another shed, I watched the sails being stitched and the ropes being stretched and spliced, ready to hold the ship's masts and sails high up above the deck.

Then, just after New Year's Day, I finally saw a ship outside my window. The roof of the shed was lifted off and there was *Duyfken*, sitting in the shadows. It was like watching a butterfly emerging from its cocoon.

Over the next few weeks, work on the ship never stopped, and lights burned brightly all night. From my window I could see the shadows of workers as they moved swiftly around the deck, getting ready for the launch of the ship.

Just before the big day, a huge, red truck arrived with a long, low trailer. The truck slowly and carefully backed into the yard and the trailer slid under the keel of the ship. When everything was ready, the truck began crawling forward.

At last the little dove was leaving the nest.

The following day, I walked in the parade alongside Bill and our team of ship-builders as we proudly led *Duyfken* through the city streets toward its launching place.

Then, as the crowd watched, *Duyfken* was lowered into the water.

The first thing I do when I get up in the morning is go to my window. But now when I look toward the sea, I think about our little ship on its very own voyage of discovery.

Glossary

bow	the front of a ship
caulking	packing the gaps between the planks with waterproof material to stop leaking
fleet	a group of ships
gun ports	the doors on the sides of a ship which open so that the guns can fire
helm	the entire apparatus for steering a ship
hull	the body of the ship
keel	the spine or base of a ship that sits below the water
masts	the large vertical poles which hold up the spars and sails
rudder	the part of a ship that steers it through the water
spars	small poles to which the sails are attached
spliced	when two ropes are joined together by twisting the smaller strands of rope into one
stern	the back of a ship
whipstaff	the lever that is used instead of a steering wheel to turn the rudder

Visit the *Duyfken* website at www.duyfken.com.